PIGLET and PAPA

written by

MARGARET

WILD

illustrated by

STEPHEN

MICHAEL

KING

HAPPY CAT BOOKS

For Olivia and her dad – M.W.

For Nicholas – S.M.K.

Published by
HAPPY CAT BOOKS
An imprint of Catnip Publishing Ltd
14 Greville Street
London EC1N 8SB

This edition first published 2008
1 3 5 7 9 10 8 6 4 2

First published in Australia in 2007 by Working Title Press, 33 Balham Avenue, Kingswood, SA 5062

Text copyright © Margaret Wild 2007
Illustrations copyright © Stephen Michael King 2007

The moral rights of the author and illustrator have been asserted

A CIP catalogue record for this book is available from the British Library

ISBN 978-1-905117-77-2

Printed in Singapore

www.catnippublishing.co.uk

Piglet loved playing with her papa.

One morning, she sat
on his head,

bounced on
his belly,

and chewed his tail. Hard.

"Ouch!" said Papa. "You little rascal!"
And he chased her out of the sty.

Piglet wasn't sure if he was
really, really cross.
"Do you love me?"
she asked in a small voice,

but Papa was grunting so loudly
he didn't hear.

Piglet crept away.

She saw Horse.

"Hello, Horse," said Piglet.
"Do you love me?"

"I like your cute little ears," said Horse,
"and I do love you —
but someone else loves you
ten times more."

"Who's that?" asked Piglet,
but Horse just smiled
as she swished away the flies.

So Piglet went on her way.

She saw Sheep.

"Hello, Sheep," said Piglet.
"Do you love me?"

"I like your snub little nose," said Sheep,
"and I do love you —
but someone else loves you
a hundred times more."

"Who's that?" asked Piglet,
but Sheep just smiled
as he munched the grass.

So Piglet went on her way.

She saw Donkey.

"Hello, Donkey," said Piglet.
"Do you love me?"

"I like your curly-whirly tail," said Donkey,
"and I do love you —
but someone else loves you
a thousand times more."

"Who's that?" asked Piglet,
but Donkey just smiled
as he kicked up his heels.

So Piglet went on her way.

She saw Duck.

"Hello, Duck," said Piglet.
"Do you love me?"

"I like your little pink trotters," said Duck,
"and I do love you —
but someone else loves you
a million times more."

"Who's that?" asked Piglet,
but Duck just smiled
as she flapped her wings.

So Piglet went on her way.

She saw Dog.

"Hello, Dog," said Piglet.
"Do you love me?"

"I like your fat little tummy," said Dog,
"and I do love you —
but someone else loves you
a billion times more."

"Who's that?" asked Piglet,
but Dog just smiled
as he dug up a bone.

Piglet was tired.
She wanted food and a hug.

So she went back to the sty —
and there was Papa waiting for her.

"Hello, Papa," said Piglet.
"Do you love me?"

"I like your cute little ears," said Papa,
"and your snub little nose and
your curly-whirly tail and your little pink
trotters and your fat little tummy."

"And?" said Piglet.

"And I love you best of all in the whole wide world!"

"I knew *that!*" said Piglet,
and she sat on her papa's head,

bounced on
his belly,

and chewed his tail —
gently.